Stickybeak

Written by Hazel Edwards
Illustrated by Rosemary Wilson

Puffin Books

Just for this weekend, Stickybeak is my pet.
From Monday to Friday, he lives in a box at school.

Everyone at school talks a lot.
So does Stickybeak.
'QUACK, QUACK, QUACK.'

We looked after three duck's eggs.
But only one duck grew.
It thought we were its parents.

The class voted for its name.
  Donald had 20 votes.
  Fluffy had 6 votes.
  Danny had 2 votes.

But Mrs Pappas said, 'Donald is a cartoon duck.
Our duck is different. We'll call him Stickybeak.'

On Friday, it was my turn.
I took Stickybeak home in a box.
We put the seatbelt around him.

'What do ducks eat?' asked Mum.
She doesn't like pets very much.
'Cornflakes,' I said.
'QUACK, QUACK, QUACK,' said Stickybeak.

At the supermarket, frozen duck was on SPECIAL.
'Not this weekend,' said Mum.

At home, Stickybeak quacked all the time.
And he messed his box too.

After dinner, I put fresh newspaper and water in his box.

'Where's my newspaper?' complained Mum.
'I haven't read the news yet.'

'Sorry Mum, Stickybeak's using it.'

Mum didn't like it much
when I gave Stickybeak a swim in our bath.

The next day, she did offer him a snail from the garden.
Stickybeak didn't like it.

'Snails have been eating my mail,' said Mum.
'I thought Stickybeak might like to be useful.'
But Stickybeak was not useful.

David-Next-Door has a lead for his dog.
I made a lead for Stickybeak.

On Sunday, we took Stickybeak to the Botanic Gardens.
Other ducks live there, on the lake.

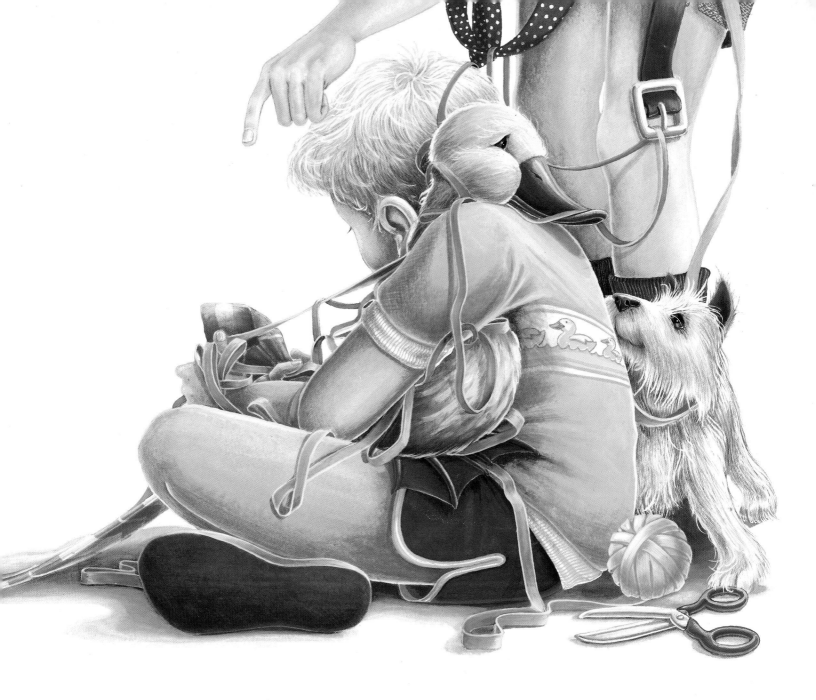

The big ducks came to meet Stickybeak.
He ran away.

In the Botanic Gardens,
a wedding party was taking videos of the bride.

Dragging his lead, Stickybeak ran quacking through their video.

Soon the bride's friends and relatives
will see Stickybeak on their videos.
They will hear him too.
'QUACK, QUACK, QUACK.'

Mum laughed as we chased Stickybeak through the gardens.

On Sunday night, Mum tried to watch the television news.
'QUACK, QUACK, QUACK.'
Stickybeak wouldn't shut up.

Mum said, 'I'm glad tomorrow is a school day.'

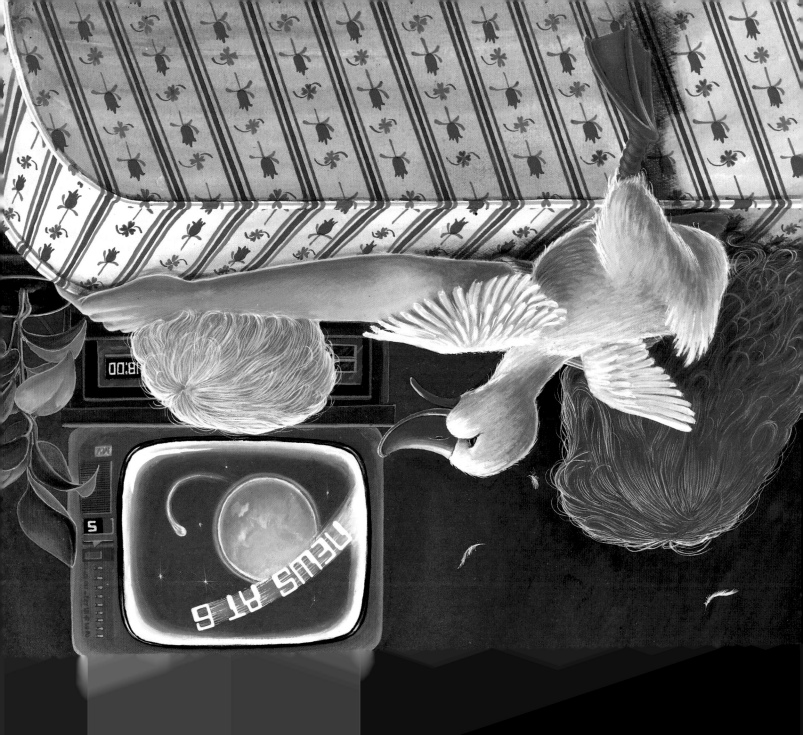

We didn't tell Mum that Mrs Pappas has a pet snake too!